THOMAS & FRIENDS™

MOVIE THEATER

Storybook & Movie Projector

Contents

studio fun

A READER'S DIGEST COMPANY

White Plains, New York • Montréal, Québec • Bath, United Kingdom

THOMAS AND THE EMERGENCY CABLE

Disk 1

Thomas loved to work on his Branch Line, pulling his faithful coaches, Annie and Clarabel.

Every day, Annie and Clarabel watched passengers board the train at Knapford Station.

Thomas watched them, too. One day, he saw a man with binoculars get on the train. He, Annie, and Clarabel saw this man a lot. He always looked through his binoculars as soon as the train left the station.

Thomas pulled into Dryaw Station. He watched the man get off.

"He's been traveling up and down the Branch Line, getting on and off at every station," said Clarabel. They all wondered who the man was.

Later that day, Thomas saw the man again. He asked him why he rode the train so often.

"I'm a bird-watcher," the man told Thomas. "And I'm trying to find a very rare bird!"

"Oh," said Thomas. "Of course!"

Thomas was hurrying along his Branch Line, when suddenly, he screeched to a halt. Someone had pulled the emergency brake!

It was the bird-watcher! "I'm sorry," he said. "I thought I heard the sound of a very rare bird . . . and I wanted to see it. . . ."

Everyone glared at him.

Soon, Thomas was on the move again. But Annie had a flat wheel. She had to be left behind.

At the next station, a cross Sir Topham Hatt scolded the bird-watcher. "The emergency cable must only be pulled when there is a genuine emergency," he said.

The bird-watcher was very sorry.

Thomas and Clarabel traveled up and down the Branch Line while Annie was being fixed. They missed her and blamed the bird-watcher.

When Thomas saw him waiting for the train, he sped right past him.

Now Sir Topham Hatt was cross with Thomas. "You must stop at every station and pick up every passenger," he said.

"I'm sorry, Sir," said Thomas.

Before long, Annie was back to work. As for the bird-watcher? He finally found his rare bird!

THOMAS THE QUARRY ENGINE

One day there was a big order of stone to be taken from the Quarry to Brendam Docks. Thomas and Diesel had been sent to collect it.

Thomas said he could pull the trucks of stone by himself. "Don't make me laugh!" said Diesel.

They did not agree on which of them should be the back engine, either.

Mavis, who worked at the Quarry, urged them to stop arguing.

Disk 2

"You two don't know how lucky you are!" Mavis said. "I work here in the Quarry all the time. You get to see the rest of Sodor . . . and the seaside!"

Diesel convinced Mavis to go to the seaside with him. They left Thomas behind to get the empty trucks loaded and ready to go to the Docks by four o'clock. The trucks were troublesome and gave Thomas a hard time.

After a while, Thomas began to get impatient. He was ready for Mavis and Diesel to come back.

"Sir Topham Hatt will be very cross if these trucks don't get to the Docks on time," he said. "But he will be very happy if I take them myself. That's it! I'll show Diesel that I don't need a back engine after all."

The Troublesome Trucks told Thomas that was a great idea. "Do it, Thomas! We won't push and we won't hold back. We'll be on our very best behavior," the Troublesome Trucks said with a laugh.

The trucks were heavy and hard to pull without a back engine. But once they were rolling, they went very well . . . until they reached the first hill!

"Hold back! Hold back!" the Troublesome Trucks said as they laughed.

Without a back engine to push from behind, it was very hard to pull the heavy trucks up the hill.

"Oh!" said Thomas, puffing and straining. "You said you were going to be good!"

"Sorry, Thomas. We forgot. We won't hold you back anymore," the trucks said. But just at that moment, Thomas began to go downhill.

"What? No . . . WAIT!!!" shouted Thomas.

Without a back engine to hold back from behind, it was very hard to slow down.

"Faster! Faster!" cried the Troublesome Trucks.

Thomas barreled forward, unable to stop. A
Signalman saw what was happening. He switched
Thomas over to a track that ended in a buffer.

Disk 3

Crash! Thomas hit the buffer and stopped. The
Troublesome Trucks behind him smashed into one
another.

 Just then, Mavis and Diesel returned. They were shocked that Thomas had tried to move the Troublesome Trucks without a back engine.

When Sir Topham Hatt arrived at the station, he was not amused.

"I know Diesel and Mavis left you all on your own, Thomas," he said. "But you should never have taken those trucks without a back engine."

"I'm sorry, Sir," said Thomas. "I was trying to be useful."

Sir Topham Hatt sent Mavis back to the Quarry to do what she did best—deal with Troublesome Trucks. But he also realized that now and then, it was nice for her to take trucks down to the Docks. That made Diesel a little bit jealous. But it made Mavis, Thomas, and all the other engines very happy indeed.

NOT SO SLOW COACHES

One day, Thomas sped up as he chugged down the tracks. Behind him, his usually faithful coaches, Annie and Clarabel, began to complain.

Disk 4

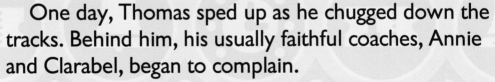

"He's doing it again, Clarabel," said Annie.

"I agree! He's going dreadfully fast," said Clarabel.

Thomas heard them. Trying to be funny, he slowed way down. Then he sped up again.

By the time Thomas arrived at Dryaw Station, he was running rather late.

"Cinders and ashes!" he cried and sped out of the station at top speed.

Annie and Clarabel squealed in displeasure.

Meanwhile, Caitlin was pulling into the train yard. Caitlin was a very fast train. In fact, she had been going so fast, she had loosened some of her bolts! She needed to leave her coaches in the yard while she went to the Steamworks to get the bolts fixed.

 As Caitlin pulled away, Thomas arrived at the train yard with Annie and Clarabel.

"Sorry, Annie and Clarabel," Thomas said. "I'll have to leave you here for a while, with Charlie. I'm late for the Quarry."

As soon as his coaches were uncoupled, Thomas hurried off to the Quarry as fast as he could go.

He picked up empty trucks from Mavis and rushed back to the train yard. But Caitlin had arrived there first to collect her coaches.

Caitlin sped down the tracks, her coaches behind her. But Charlie had accidentally hooked Annie and Clarabel to Caitlin, too.

A sleepy Annie and Clarabel awakened to discover they were hurtling down the tracks faster than they had ever gone before!

Disk 5

They saw Thomas on the track way behind them. Just when they thought things couldn't get worse, they heard Caitlin challenge Connor to a race to Ulfstead Castle. And, he agreed!

"NO!" cried Annie and Clarabel as they were pulled along at high speed.

"NO!" called Thomas, who was racing down the tracks as fast he could go to catch up to Caitlin. But the little steam engine could not match the speed of the streamlined engine.

"I'll never complain about Thomas again!" Clarabel called out.

"Nor will I!" Annie shouted.

"If I ever get Annie and Clarabel back, I'll never tease them again," said Thomas as he hurried after Caitlin and Connor. The two streamlined engines were so far ahead, he could no longer see them.

Suddenly, Caitlin sped past Thomas going in the opposite direction! Caitlin was already on her way back. "Thomas!" she called out as she whipped past him, her coaches—and Annie and Clarabel—behind her.

Thomas hurried to stop Caitlin before she went over the Vicarstown Bridge to the Mainland. But the bridge's gate came down, and the bridge was raised just as Thomas was about to cross it. "Oh no!" he cried. "I'll never catch Caitlin now."

When the bridge was lowered, Thomas was surprised to see Hiro. He was even more surprised to see that Annie and Clarabel were with him!

"It's a good thing I stopped Caitlin," Hiro said. "She was taking away your coaches."

"Thank you!" cried a very grateful Thomas. Annie and Clarabel thanked Hiro, too.

"Oh, Annie and Clarabel, I'm sorry I teased you," said Thomas.

"And we're sorry we complained about how fast you were going," said Annie.

"We'll never do it again," added Clarabel.

Thomas was so happy to have Annie and Clarabel back, he couldn't stop smiling.